Weekly Reader Children's Book Club Presents

DANNY DUNN

and the

Swamp Monster

DANNY DUNN
and the
Swamp Monster

by Jay Williams and Raymond Abrashkin

Illustrated by Paul Sagsoorian

McGRAW-HILL BOOK COMPANY

New York · Toronto · London · Sydney
St. Louis · San Francisco · Mexico · Panama

Also by Jay Williams and Raymond Abrashkin

DANNY DUNN AND THE ANTI-GRAVITY PAINT
DANNY DUNN AND THE AUTOMATIC HOUSE
DANNY DUNN AND THE FOSSIL CAVE
DANNY DUNN AND THE HEAT RAY
DANNY DUNN AND THE HOMEWORK MACHINE
DANNY DUNN ON A DESERT ISLAND
DANNY DUNN ON THE OCEAN FLOOR
DANNY DUNN AND THE WEATHER MACHINE
DANNY DUNN TIME TRAVELER
DANNY DUNN AND THE VOICE FROM SPACE
DANNY DUNN AND THE SMALLIFYING MACHINE

ACKNOWLEDGMENTS
The authors wish to express their gratitude for special advice and assistance to Leo Bennett, Chairman of Universal Control Equipment Ltd., Stroud; to John Atwood, of Perkin-Elmer, Inc., and to the Press Officer, Republic of Sudan, London. For material about the Nuer, who are a little-known and very independent people, I am indebted to the researches and writings of E. E. Evans Pritchard.

Contents

1 A Message in Code   7
2 The Superconductor   17
3 A Trial of Strength   28
4 On the Track of a Legend   37
5 A Warm Christmas Present   48
6 The Man in White   57
7 In the Sudd   67
8 Tracks in the Mud   77
9 On the Monitor Screen   87
10 "Sabotage!"   97
11 The Monster of the Swamp   106
12 "You Have One Hour"   116
13 Danny Finds an Answer   125
14 The Invisible Barrier   130
15 Farewell to the *Lau*   138

ONE

A Message in Code

Professor Euclid Bullfinch frowned through his glasses at the small piece of paper in his hand.

"REGRET IMPOSSIBLE KHARTOUMWARDS EX-WEEKS STOP SEVERAL PROBLEMS REQUIRE AMERICAN VISIT BOTHERATION WILL COMMUNICATE," it said.

The red-haired, freckled boy, reading it over his shoulder, pursed his lips in a soundless whistle.

"I don't get it, Professor," he said. "What does it mean?"

"Hard to tell, Danny," said the Professor. "But the main problem is, who is it from?"

He examined the envelope it had come in. It had the name of the Amstel Hotel in Amsterdam printed on it, and Professor Bullfinch's name and address typed on the front. There was a Netherlands airmail stamp on it.

"Whom do I know in Amsterdam?" murmured the Professor.

"Maybe it's a mistake," Danny said.

"Aha!" Professor Bullfinch nodded. "A very shrewd suggestion, my boy. It is certainly a mistake. Whoever sent it must also have typed out a telegram he meant to send someone else. Then he put the text of the telegram in this envelope instead of the letter. So we know two things about him. He must be rather absent-minded. And he must be well-to-do because the Amstel is the best hotel in Amsterdam."

He rubbed his chin pensively. "Two clues. Absent-minded and rich. But still not enough."

At that moment, the front doorbell rang. The Professor crammed the puzzling letter into a pocket of his old tweed jacket and went to the door. He returned after a moment with a large square package.

"It was the messenger from the chemical plant," he said. "These are the new materials I ordered. Now I'll be able to complete my experiment."

"Can I watch?" Dan asked.

"Certainly. Come along," said the Professor, leading the way down the corridor to the back of the house.

Danny's father had died when the boy was only a baby, and Mrs. Dunn had had to look for a job to support herself and the child. She had found a post as housekeeper for Professor Bullfinch. The Professor, a world-famous scientist, lived in the university town of Midston. His many inventions had brought him enough money to maintain a private laboratory where he conducted his experiments. He treated Dan as if he were his own son, and the boy's interest in science had grown until his knowledge of many aspects of it was greater than that of most grownups.

The lab was a large room facing the back lawn and garden. It was filled with all sorts of equipment, had its own library, and was even connected by a direct teletype machine to the giant computer at Midston University. The Professor set the package down on one of the lab benches and unwrapped it. Inside, in a well-padded box, were four small glass jars full of liquid, each of a different color.

"These substances, which I have developed and which the plant manufactured for me," explained the Professor, "will unite to form a polymer resin plastic. I believe I can produce something with special qualities of lightness and strength."

He arranged a piece of apparatus on the bench. Its central part was a metal container surrounded by a wire grid and supported on four long legs. A small nozzle opened in the bottom. The Professor hooked up a length of cable to the wire grid. Then he poured the contents of the four jars into the container.

He touched a switch. A faint humming came from the wires. The container began to revolve slowly.

"We have a little time while the stuff cooks and mixes," said the Professor. "Meanwhile, let's look at that peculiar letter again."

He pulled it from his pocket and smoothed it out on the lab bench. Danny rested his chin on his hands, his elbows on the bench, and read the message aloud.

"What do you suppose this word means?" he asked. "K— Kartum—"

"Khartoum," said the Professor. "It's a city in the Sudan, in Central Africa. Khartoumwards means 'to Khartoum.' It's cablese."

"What's that? An African language?"

Professor Bullfinch chuckled. "No, cablese is the special language used by people who send a lot of messages by telegraph. Newspaper reporters, for instance. When you send a message by radio, or by the Atlantic cable, you have to pay for every word. So reporters have developed a special shorthand way of saying things. For instance, instead of saying 'to me,' which would be two words, they say, 'mewards' which is only one."

"That means that whoever wrote this message must have been a reporter!" Danny exclaimed.

"Perhaps. Or he could have been someone who sends a lot of telegrams. Someone who travels a good deal."

"To places like Central Africa."

"Just so. Distant places." Professor Bullfinch tapped the paper on his palm. "There's another clue in this message. What does a scientist use to show an unknown quantity?"

"An x," Danny said.

"The message says 'exweeks.' An unknown number of weeks. So this man is a scientist—"

"And he's sending the message to another scientist," Danny finished. "Someone who would also know what 'exweeks' meant."

The Professor snapped his fingers triumphantly. "Correct! And I've just thought of another thing. Now the pieces fall into place. I think I can guess—but I must just make a phone call." He hurried to the door. "Keep an eye on the cooking pot. If the warning light goes on, shut off the power."

He went out, leaving Danny to eye the revolving container.

"I forgot to ask him which light is the warning light," Dan mused. "Let's see. This must be the temperature dial. This light is green so that must mean the current is running into this wire—"

He was interrupted by a sudden loud thump and a rattle of glass behind him. He swung round.

Between two large windows, a glass-paned door led into the garden. Just outside stood a smallish man with a weather-beaten face and a wild white beard. He was rubbing his forehead in a dazed way.

Danny ran to open the door. "Were you knocking?" he asked.

12

"No, no," said the man. "Don't mention it. I'm sorry. I seem to have walked into your door."

He stepped forward and took Dan's hand. "How are you, old friend?" he asked, shaking it warmly.

Danny stared at him open-mouthed. The bearded man's eyes were curiously blank. He looked at Danny as if not really seeing him.

"I'm—I'm fine, I guess," Danny gulped. "How are you?"

"It's been a long time," the man went on. "Years and years. You haven't changed a bit."

Then, as abruptly as if someone had turned a switch, his eyes seemed to come into focus. He blinked at Danny.

"But you have!" he exclaimed. "You've changed a lot. In fact, you're not you at all."

"What do you mean?" Danny began backing away in alarm. "Of course I'm me. Who do you think I am?"

"Well, I really can't say who you are," said the man. "If *you* don't know, how do you expect me to know? We've never met. Or have we? You see," he said, coming into the lab and leaning comfortably against a bench, "I meet so many people. And I'm afraid as I get older, my memory gets worse. Have we met?"

14

"Why, er—no—I don't think so," Danny stammered.

The man was wearing a strange, wide-brimmed hat with a leopard-skin band. He took it off and began fanning himself with it.

"That's a relief," he said. "But really, my boy, you ought to pull yourself together. See a doctor or something. It's pretty serious when you can't remember who you are."

"But I do remember who I are!" cried Danny, in confusion.

The man suddenly smiled. "Hello, old chap," he said, moving forward with his hand outstretched.

Danny retreated in a panic. Then, all at once, he realized that Professor Bullfinch had come back into the room. It was to him that the bearded man was speaking.

Danny went to the Professor's side.

"Professor," he whispered, "I think this man is crazy."

Professor Bullfinch patted him on the shoulder.

"I don't blame you for thinking so, Dan," he said. "I've sometimes thought so myself. But, in

15

fact, he's one of the sanest men I know. He's my old friend, Dr. Benjamin Fenster. Good to see you, Ben," he added, gripping the bearded man's hand. "I guessed it was you who sent that message."

"Of course it was me," said Dr. Fenster with a puzzled look. "Who else should I have been?"

Danny clutched at his head. "Oh, no!" he wailed. "Let's not start that again!"

TWO

The Superconductor

Dr. Fenster patted the boy gently on the shoulder.

"You seem disturbed, son," he said. "Better take an aspirin and lie down for a while."

"I don't blame him for feeling muddled," said Professor Bullfinch. "You sometimes have that effect on people, Ben. For instance, look at this. This is the message you sent me."

He handed the piece of paper to Dr. Fenster. The bearded man tossed his hat on the lab bench, and with a lightness and ease that didn't seem to go with his white hair and lined, brown face, hopped up to sit beside it. He took the paper and read it with a frown.

"You're a little muddled yourself, Euclid," he said. "This is the message I sent Professor Ismail of the University of Khartoum. How did you get hold of it?"

The Professor ran his hand wearily over his bald head. "You sent it to me," he said patiently. "You will notice that you didn't sign it. However, Dan and I were able to figure out who it came from."

Dr. Fenster broke into a merry laugh. "Good for you," he said. "How'd you manage?"

"We deduced that the sender was a scientist of some sort who did a lot of traveling and sent a lot of telegrams. I know three or four such people. Also, we knew he was absent-minded. That narrowed it down to two. Then I realized that he had to be almost supernaturally absent-minded, because he was someone who could carefully save words in a telegram and then put in an absolutely unnecessary word like 'botheration.' You're the only one I know who fits the whole description."

Dr. Fenster stroked his beard. "I hope Professor Ismail is as clever. I don't think I signed the letter, either."

"The telegram says that you're coming to America," Professor Bullfinch went on, "and I guessed that you must have written to me to say you were going to visit me. I telephoned the best hotel in town and they told me you'd registered this morning but were out. So I knew you were on your way here."

18

"Well," said Dr. Fenster, "I guess I have given you a good deal of trouble." He turned his twinkling black eyes on Dan. "I'm sorry, son. I didn't mean to mix you up."

"That's all right," said Danny. "But I really *do* know who I am. I'm Danny Dunn." They shook hands.

Professor Bullfinch said, "It's a great honor for you, Dan, to meet Dr. Fenster. He is a famous zoologist who has traveled to many out-of-the-way corners of the earth in search of strange animals. He has discovered many new species, written a dozen books, received half a dozen medals. He is known to his friends by the name some African people once gave him: *Mtu'anaye.*"

"What does it mean?" Danny asked. "Explorer? Great Hunter?"

"It means The Forgetful One," said the Professor.

"I've never met a real absent-minded professor before," Danny said. "In fact, I didn't think there were any outside of books."

"In the first place, I'm not a professor," Dr. Fenster objected. "And I'm not really absent-minded. It's just that I have a lot of things to

think about and I sometimes can only manage one at a time."

He turned to Professor Bullfinch. "That brings me to the reason for my coming," he said solemnly. "I am about to embark on one of the most interesting expeditions of my career."

"What—?" began the Professor.

He was interrupted by a shout from Danny. "Look, Professor! The plastic!"

They had forgotten all about the revolving container. It was spinning more rapidly and wobbling in a most alarming manner. A bright red light was blinking on and off. Worse yet, the nozzle at the bottom of the container had been opened by the violent spinning and a strand of dark, shining material about the thickness of ordinary string was jetting out. The wobbling motion made it fall in large coils one on top of the other on the stone surface of the workbench. The last of it fell as they watched.

"Shut off the power!" cried the Professor.

Danny shot forward, quicker than either of the men. He hesitated for an instant before the machine, not being able to find the switch that turned off the power. Then, impulsively, he made up his mind about the quickest way to do things—Danny was often given to headstrong action. He grabbed the cable and with one quick jerk yanked it free from its connections.

The container swung slowly to a halt. But the cable was still live. Danny dropped it like a snake. The bare wires at its tip landed squarely on the plastic coils. They shone with an unearthly green light.

At the same time, Professor Bullfinch had reached the power switch, which was set in a box

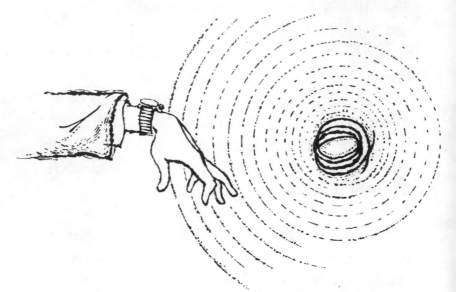

on the wall and not on the machine. He snapped it off. Then he pulled out his handkerchief and mopped his forehead.

Dr. Fenster said, "Life is pretty exciting here, Euclid. I think I prefer the peaceful jungle. What would that thing have done—exploded?"

"Oh, no," said the Professor. "Nothing like that. I was cooking up a polymer, but I'm afraid it may be ruined now."

"Why is it still glowing?" Danny asked.

"Glowing?" The Professor stared. Sure enough, from the loops of plastic came a faint but unmistakable greenish gleam.

"It's just a reflection, isn't it?" said Dr. Fenster. He had jumped down from his perch and now moved closer to look over the Professor's shoulder.

"No," answered the Professor. "Some change has taken place in the structure of the material."

He reached to pick it up. He stood motionless, his hand a foot or so from the coiled plastic cord. On his face was an odd mixture of surprise and bafflement.

"What's the matter?" Danny said. "Don't you feel well?"

"The matter?" Professor Bullfinch sounded distracted. "Very curious. Very curious, indeed. The matter is that I can't seem to get my hand any closer to the stuff than this."

"Is there something wrong with your hand?" said Dr. Fenster.

"Nothing's wrong. But—" The Professor's voice died away. Then abruptly, he said, "Is it possible?"

"Is what possible? What are you talking about?"

Without replying, Professor Bullfinch withdrew his hand. Around his wrist was a watch with a stainless-steel band. Quickly, he unfastened the band and took off the watch. Once again, he reached for the plastic. This time, his fingers touched it.

"Great heavens!" breathed Dr. Fenster. "A magnetic field! But how—?"

"Don't you see?" said the Professor. "It's a superconductor."

"But that's incredible!" Dr. Fenster said. "At room temperature—?"

"So it appears. There's no other explanation."

"A superconductor?" Danny put in. "What's that?"

Professor Bullfinch took out his pipe. He filled it from a worn pouch and deliberately lit it.

Through the cloud of smoke, he said, "Well, my boy, you know that when an electrical current passes through what's called a conductor—a wire, for instance—it meets a certain amount of resistance. This is caused by the atoms of the metal deflecting the moving electrons from their path. It has been discovered that if the material is cooled to a very low temperature, down to somewhere near absolute zero, it loses almost all its resistance. What we seem to have here, however, is a material with no resistance to an electrical current, without having to be made so cold. It's more than just an electrical conductor, it's a superconductor.

"You might think of it this way: the conductor is a road with lots of obstacles in it. The electrons carrying the charge are deflected from their path so the traffic is slowed up. But this plastic is like a wide speedway. The electrons can move in large loops and avoid all the obstacles. So they go around and around at high speed, and if the speedway is a circle, they will never stop."

"Never?" Danny gazed up at the Professor in wonder. "You mean it would be a kind of perpetual motion? But I thought that wasn't possible."

"Nevertheless, that's just what it would be."

25

Professor Bullfinch leaned forward to inspect the plastic. "Look here. The two ends of this coil are touching. It forms a closed ring. When you dropped the cable, it started a charge going through the coil. Now, my boy, a moving charge of electricity flowing around a circuit produces a magnetic field. What we have here is a very powerful ring magnet, so powerful that when I tried to touch it the magnetic field caught and held the metal of my wrist watch."

"A supermagnet," said Danny.

"That's right. And it will go on being a magnet, with the current flowing on and on around the circle until I break the current. Like this."

Professor Bullfinch glanced about. He found a pair of heavy rubber gloves and put them on. He seized the coil and pulled its two ends apart. There was a flash and a snap.

The Professor turned to Dr. Fenster. "As you can see, this means—" he was beginning.

Dr. Fenster, with a glassy, faraway look in his eyes, was walking towards the door that led to the garden.

"Ben!" Professor Bullfinch called. "What's wrong? Where are you going?"

Dr. Fenster flapped a hand. "Nice to meet you, sir," he said. "Don't call me, I'll call you."

Without another word, he pulled open the door and walked out into the garden. He was soon lost to sight in the shrubbery, leaving the Professor and Danny staring open-mouthed after him.

THREE

A Trial of Strength

Professor Bullfinch slowly closed the door. "If I know my friend Ben," he said, "he is thinking about something."

"But will he be all right?" asked Danny. "He didn't seem to know where he was."

"Oh, he'll look after himself. We'll hear from him again when he's got the problem thought out," said the Professor.

He returned to the lab bench and took up the strand of plastic. "I have some thinking of my own to do," he said. "And some experimentation as well."

Danny was about to ask whether he could stay and watch, when there came a shrill whistle from outside. In one of the windows appeared the faces of a thin, sad-looking boy and an attractive girl with her brown hair in a pony tail.

"It's Joe and Irene," Danny said. "I'll see you at lunch, Professor."

Professor Bullfinch waved to the two faces, put

28

a match to his pipe, and returned to his work.
Dan went out to join his friends.

"Where've you been?" he asked them.

"Irene's been collecting beetles for her proj-
ect," Joe Pearson said. "And I've been carrying
the beetle bottles." He was holding a box with
several glass jars in it. "I don't know why I do
it," he added gloomily. "I can't stand bugs. I
must be crazy."

"You're just kindhearted," Irene Miller
chuckled. "And also greedy. My mother made

an angel cake with coffee frosting. I promised him some if he'd help me," she told Danny.

"Speaking of crazy," said Joe, "we just passed a very peculiar-looking character. A little man, not much taller than me, with a white beard. He was muttering to himself and walking around in circles in the field on the other side of those trees. When we passed him, we said hello, and he nodded and said, 'Yes, it is, isn't it?' I was just wondering whether we ought to call the hospital or someplace."

"Not necessary. He's a friend of Professor Bullfinch's," said Danny. "He's sort of absent-minded. He was here just now when the Professor made his newest invention."

"What invention?"

"Well, it's a kind of magnet."

"What's so special about that?" Joe said. "Magnets have already been invented."

"No, this is something new. It's really a super-conductor which offers no resistance to current . . ."

"Never mind," Joe groaned. "I can see I'm not going to understand a word of it."

Irene, who was as interested in science as Dan,

patted Joe's shoulder. "You don't have to listen," she said. "You can write a poem about it later. Go ahead, Dan. Tell me."

Danny explained as best he could. "So you see," he finished, "it doesn't just pull things or push them, the way a bar magnet does. Since it's in the shape of a ring, it produces a circular magnetic field. It held the Professor's wrist watch so that he couldn't even move his hand."

"It must be very powerful," said Irene.

Dan nodded. "I've been thinking about things that could be done with it," he said. "And I've got a couple of ideas."

"Here we go," Joe said. "He's got that look in his eye that means, 'Help me with this new idea and we'll all get into trouble.' The last one was to rig a steam drive to my bike. I'm still finding pieces of it in my back yard."

"This is nothing like that," Danny said. "For instance, if you mounted one of these superconductor magnets on the front of a car, you could never crash into another car."

"That's a terrific idea," said Irene.

"I'll bet it wouldn't work that way," Joe said gloomily. "Something would go wrong and you'd have a million cars all stuck together forever."

Danny shook his head. "You don't understand —" he was beginning when there came a sound of running feet. The three youngsters turned.

Dr. Fenster came galloping along, waving his hat. "Eureka!" he cried. "Where's Euclid? I've got it!"

"Got what?" said Joe nervously. "Is it something catching?"

Dr. Fenster glanced at him in surprise. "You're different," he said. "You used to be a red-headed, freckled boy and now you're tall, skinny, and black-haired."

He pushed past Joe, leaving him staring open-mouthed, and barged through the laboratory door. Danny and the others followed.

Professor Bullfinch looked up calmly. "Ah, Ben," he said, "got it all worked out, whatever it was?"

"I think so, Euclid. Just one question, first. What's the total weight of that coil of plastic?"

The Professor raised his eyebrows. He took a brass scales from a shelf, set it on the bench, and put the hank of dark plastic cord on it.

"About forty-six grams, or an ounce and a half. Do you want me to be more precise?"

"No, that'll do. That stuff has a diameter of less than half a centimeter, or about a sixteenth of an inch, right? Let's see how tough it is. I just want a rough notion. Can we hang up a piece of it and see how much weight it will support, for example?"

"Certainly." Professor Bullfinch looked around the laboratory. There were some hooks along one wall on which overalls and rubber aprons were hanging. He cut off a few feet of the plastic cord and tied one end of it to one of the hooks. He made a loop in the other end.

"Now, what shall we use for a weight?" he asked.

"Use me," said Dr. Fenster. "I weigh about a hundred and thirty pounds. All right?"

"Yes, of course."

Dr. Fenster promptly put one foot in the loop. He reached up to hold the hook so that he could steady himself. Then, slowly, he let himself down until his weight was all on the foot resting in that fragile-looking loop of plastic. To the watchers, it seemed as though the cord must

break. It stretched a trifle, but it held him as if it were heavy rope.

He got down briskly. "Good," he said. "That's all I need to know right now. I think this may provide the very solution I came here to find."

"What was that?" asked the Professor.

"I didn't know. But now I think I do."

"You're being confusing again, Ben. What does all that mean?"

"Just what I've been wondering," said a new voice. "What on earth is going on?"

It was Danny's mother, Mrs. Dunn. She stood in the doorway, a lock of red hair hanging over her eyes.

"Well," she said. "You're quite a little convention in here, aren't you? Still, I suppose I can find room for all of you around the table."

"You don't mean to say it's lunch time already?" said the Professor.

"I've been calling you for the past five minutes," said Mrs. Dunn. "Hello, Joe, Irene. Just run in and phone your mothers. There's plenty to eat. And I don't believe I've met this gentleman."

The Professor introduced Dr. Fenster. The zoologist made Mrs. Dunn a dignified bow.

"Delighted to meet you, ma'am," he said. "Your invitation to lunch is gratefully accepted. I can't seem to remember eating breakfast."

"He really *is* absent-minded," Joe whispered to Danny. "Imagine not being able to remember eating!"

"Let's go, then," said the Professor, clapping Dr. Fenster on the back. "And after lunch, you can tell us all about this mysterious problem of yours."

FOUR

On the Track of a Legend

Lunch was what Mrs. Dunn called a pick-up meal. "I just pick up whatever's around the kitchen and put it on the table," she said. What she had picked up today was a gigantic chicken salad, cold baked ham, hot biscuits with home-made strawberry jam, and an apple pie with bits of cinnamon stick under the juicy crust.

"I haven't eaten so much," puffed Dr. Fenster, pushing his chair away from the table, "since a three-day feast the Pygmies once gave me."

"What did you have?" Joe asked.

"It began with roast elephant," said Dr. Fenster.

"I don't know whether to say 'yum' or 'ugh,' " Joe said.

"It was delicious," Dr. Fenster assured him.

"Oh, Joe!" said Irene. "How can you talk about eating right after a meal like that?"

"I'm talented," he replied cheerfully. "That

reminds me. You owe me some angel cake with coffee frosting."

"Oog! He's hopeless," Irene groaned.

Mrs. Dunn giggled and began to clear the table. Dr. Fenster lit a long, thin cigar, and the Professor tamped down the tobacco in his pipe with a calloused thumb.

"Now, Ben," he said, digging out his matches, "let's hear your story."

Dr. Fenster settled himself more comfortably in his chair.

"Well," he began, "you know I am always in touch with people all over the world, from whom I often hear of new or strange animals. Sometimes, the natives of a place will have legends or tales about weird beasts, and sometimes it turns out that there's a good deal of truth behind them. Many scientists tend to pooh-pooh such tales, but I think myself that the people who live in a place know better than any outsider what's there. For instance, way back in 1860 the Wambutti people in the Congo told explorers about a zebra-striped, long-eared creature that lived in the jungles. Nobody believed them. But eventually the beast was discovered. It's the okapi, a relative of the giraffe. The same thing has been true of other animals—the monster dragon-lizard of Komodo, the pygmy hippopotamus of Liberia, and the great black Ituri boar.

"Well, now I'm on the track of just such another legend. And I hope it may turn out to be just as real an animal."

He tapped the long ash off his cigar. The others waited in silent fascination. He regarded them gravely, and continued:

"You know that the River Nile rises in Uganda, in Central Africa, and flows almost four thousand miles north to its outlet in Egypt. About a quarter of the way from its source, it winds among swamps—nine thousand square miles of them—watery, wild, with few people living there, an area that's almost unexplored. I have passed through the region several times, and last year I spent a week in the town of Malakal with an old friend of mine, Ibrahim Ajay. There I heard for the first time the stories about the *lau*.

"The Nuer people who live in the swamps say that the *lau* is a serpent, bigger than any other.

Its body is as big around as a horse. Its color is brown, like the mud, and on its head are long tentacles. It reaches out with these to seize its victims. And the Nuer say, 'If a man sees the *lau* first, the serpent dies, but if the *lau* sees the man first, the man dies.' "

"Goodness!" exclaimed Mrs. Dunn. "It sounds frightful. But surely, it's just a legend? You don't really believe there is such a beast, do you?"

"Yes," said Dr. Fenster solemnly, "I do."

"Because of what you said before—that the natives of a country know best what animals live there?" said Danny.

"Right. Reports of the *lau* go back for many years. In 1923, H. C. Jackson, Deputy Governor of the Upper Nile Province, said that the Nuer people had told him about the creature. The great naturalist, J. G. Millais, heard about it; so did the Government Administrator at Rejaf; so did the explorer, Captain William Hitchens. And my friend Ibrahim told me that he had seen the track of the *lau* near the village of Yakwak. It was a huge channel deep in the mud and

40

wide enough, he said, for four men to lie down in."

Joe snorted. "But how can you believe that stuff about, 'If a man sees the *lau* first, the *lau* dies, but if the *lau* sees the man first, the man dies'?" He said. "It's like the old myth about the Gorgon who turned people to stone if they looked at her. Gosh, you don't believe *she* ever existed, do you?"

Dr. Fenster ran his fingers through his beard. Then he said, "Do you know what a metaphor is?"

"Sure he does," Irene put in. "He's a poet."

"Splendid. Well, then, suppose I told you, 'I saw something so horrible yesterday that it froze my blood.' You wouldn't think my blood really turned to ice, would you?"

"I suppose not," said Joe. "You mean the Gorgon didn't really turn men to stone, but just scared them stiff."

"Just so, scared them stiff as stone. Now let's put it another way. If you were walking through the jungle and you met a cobra, and you came very close to it without seeing it, it might bite you and then you'd be dead. But if you saw it first, you'd kill it before it could harm you. Right?"

"I get it. Of course!" Joe said. "It's just a kind of poetic way of telling about something."

"Then you think the *lau* may be a poisonous snake?" said Danny.

"Not necessarily," Dr. Fenster answered. "Just dangerous. Not even a snake—it might be an enormous crocodile. Or a creature like a crocodile, a giant lizard for instance—"

"Or a dinosaur!" Danny said. "It might be a dinosaur still alive in the swamps."

Dr. Fenster shrugged. "I don't know. But I feel sure it's *something*. Something new which has not yet been discovered. And I hope to discover it."

Professor Bullfinch had been listening intently with his chin on his hand. He said, "There's only one thing I don't understand, Ben. You said you came here to see me because you had a problem. How on earth can I help you find a strange animal? I don't know anything about animal catching. I've never even been to Africa."

"Yes, but you are full of ideas. I came to toss

questions at you and see what you'd come up with. The problem is that it is very difficult to move about in the Nile swamps at any time, and almost impossible at night. Yet I want to be able to keep a large section of swampland under constant observation, day and night."

"Big searchlights?" Danny suggested.

"The lights might scare the creature away."

"What about a television camera, one that can see in the dark?" said Irene.

"Exactly my thought," said Dr. Fenster. "Not one, but several such cameras. The problem is one of weight. I'd need special small cameras. But heavy cables, lots of them, long enough to do the job, would weigh far too much. And that's where this new plastic of yours comes in, Euclid. As soon as I understood what it was, I began to see the possibilities.

"It is a superconductor of electricity. It's very strong and tough. And it weighs almost nothing. That means that from a base camp I could set out hundreds of feet of it, to the cameras. It would have to be insulated, of course."

"Not necessarily," said the Professor. "But a protective coat of some kind of paint—"

"And the miniature TV cameras—?"

"Yes, that would be perfectly possible."

"Another serious problem is that the ground is covered with fifteen-foot-high papyrus. I'd somehow have to get the cameras up above the stuff. Cranes, or poles, would be too heavy to carry in and too hard to set up, since the ground is so soft."

They frowned at each other. Then Danny cried, "I know! You could hang them in the air."

"Eh? I don't follow," said Dr. Fenster.

"On balloons!" Danny grinned.

"By George, I believe the lad's got something," said Dr. Fenster. "What a good idea! Since our electrical cables won't weigh anything to speak of, it could be done."

He stood up, leaned across the table, and shook hands with Danny. "Well done. I could use a bright boy like you on this expedition," he said.

Danny's eyes glowed. "Really?" he said. "Do you mean it?"

"Why not?" Dr. Fenster tugged at his beard and laughed. "You all ought to come. You especially, Euclid. I need your inventive brain. And

what a time I'd show you! Never been to Africa?
A fantastic place. An unforgettable experience!"

"You're not serious, Ben?" said the Professor.

"Never been more serious in my life."

"But the expense—"

"Now, now, Euclid. You know I have more
money than I know what to do with. It won't
cost you a penny."

"Gosh!" said Joe. "Are you really that rich?"

Dr. Fenster nodded. "I'm even rarer than
most of the animals I search for. I'm the only
millionaire zoologist there is."

"Oh, boy!" said Danny. "Africa!"

"But wouldn't it be dangerous?" asked Irene.
"I mean, lions and crocodiles and poisonous
snakes—"

"There aren't any lions where we'd be going,"
answered Dr. Fenster. "As for crocodiles, you
just have to use common sense and not swim
where they swim. And you have poisonous
snakes right here, around Midston. There are
copperheads and rattlers up in the hills, aren't
there? Yet that doesn't stop you from hiking."

"No, of course not. Oh, wouldn't it be marvel-
lous if we could all go!"

"No reason why you shouldn't," said Dr. Fenster heartily. "Just as soon as we get all the details ironed out. We'll fly to Khartoum first, and then I'll charter a big amphibian—"

"Just a moment." Mrs. Dunn's voice was sharp. They all looked at her. She stood, arms folded, wearing the kind of expression Danny

46

knew well from the times when he'd done something more than usually thoughtless.

"Are you serious about this hare-brained expedition?" she demanded.

"Perfectly serious, ma'am," said Dr. Fenster.

"You are really considering taking these three youngsters and the Professor along with you into the depths of some sort of horrible swamp?"

"But it's not horrible," Dr. Fenster said.

She cut him short.

"Professor Bullfinch can, of course, make up his own mind," she said. "And I don't know what the Pearsons and the Millers will decide. But as far as I'm concerned, the very last thing I'd ever permit would be for Danny to go on such a long and frightful trip. And that's final!"

FIVE

A Warm Christmas Present

The plane circled and began its long slant towards the airstrip. Water sparkled below, and the square roofs of houses made a checkerboard pattern off to one side. Dr. Fenster glanced through the window.

"That's the Nile," he said. "Or rather, both Niles—the White and the Blue. They meet at Khartoum."

"They both look the same color from here," said Joe.

The three young people were craning their necks, trying to see all they could in spite of being constrained by their seat belts.

"You'll find that they really are different colors, though," said Dr. Fenster. "One is brownish-white and the other blue-gray. It's because of the kind of soil they travel through to get here."

"We may not have much time for seeing their colors," Professor Bullfinch warned. "The chil-

dren have only two weeks. You remember what we promised their parents."

The trip had been a Christmas present.

For a long time, the Millers and the Pearsons had felt as Mrs. Dunn did that the whole idea of their children going halfway around the world to search for some possibly dangerous animal in a savage land was out of the question. But little by little, Dr. Fenster had talked them over. From the start, he had had the help of Professor Bullfinch, who was as eager to go as the children themselves, and who joined his voice to that of the zoologist. Dr. Fenster said that he had lived and worked in Africa for many years and that

the region he was going to was no more dangerous than most American forests or swamps like
the Everglades, or Yellowstone Park. The expedition would have plenty of supplies, and he
himself knew a good deal about medicine—he
had to, since he often went deep into the bush
on his journeys and was a long way from doctors
and hospitals. There were, in the swampland of
the Sudd, few wild animals. The people were
easy to deal with. In case of emergency, his own
chartered amphibious plane would be at hand.
To hear him talk, it was as safe as if he were pro-
posing a stroll in Midston Park, and to cap it all
off he insisted that the trip would cost nothing.
In the end, Mrs. Dunn had given her consent,
and once she had agreed to let Danny go, the
Pearsons and the Millers had no peace until
they, too, gave in.

Dr. Fenster said that the best time for his expedition was the dry season, which began in No-
vember. By that time, too, the special equipment would all be ready. So it was decided that
they would set out right after Christmas, and
that the children could have two full weeks
from the time of their arrival in Khartoum. At

the end of that time, however, whether there was any result or not, they would be put on a plane and sent home. "I know my Danny," Mrs. Dunn remarked. "He won't want to leave until Dr. Fenster gives up, and that might not be for a year or more."

All the Christmas presents had been thrown a little in the shade by the trip. Still, they had admired each other's trees and had eaten themselves full of good food. Then the good-byes had been said, and all the last-minute things that had been forgotten were remembered—too late—and off they had flown on the first leg of the journey, to New York. From there, they had taken the London plane, and now, after a total of nearly twenty hours of flight, they were arriving at their destination. They had caught up on the sun; as Irene put it, "We've been flying towards yesterday."

They gathered their things together as the plane came to a halt. They went out into the blazing hot sunshine of the morning.

"I can't believe it's December," Danny said, wiping his face with one hand and struggling to hold his suitcase and overcoat with the other.

A large car was waiting for them at the airport. They all piled in. Soon, they were driving towards the city.

Suddenly, Irene shrieked, "Look! Camels!"

They were approaching the first houses, low structures of mud-brick, the color of milky coffee. And there, in a dusty square, were three or four camels, their long necks curving high so that they looked like weird swans. Veiled figures stood around them.

"Now we really know we're in a foreign land," said Danny.

They had glimpses of modern offices and shops among the old, brick, flat-topped houses; of an open air market thronged with dark-skinned people in white robes; of a mosque with a dome and tall minaret. Then they came out at the river's edge and parked before a handsome brick building. Its front was lined with arched, pointed windows, and a double row of palm trees led up to it. Other buildings could be seen behind it.

"This is Khartoum University," said Dr. Fenster, as he got out of the car.

They followed him to the stone-and-glass Col-

lege of Science, a new building. There, in a spotless but crowded laboratory, they found a wrinkled old black man, gray-haired and gray-bearded, making notes at a table on which stood a glass tank with a single fish in it.

Dr. Fenster went eagerly towards him. They hugged each other, patting each other on the back and exclaiming loudly in Arabic.

Then Dr. Fenster said, "Allow me to present my dear friend, Professor Hamid Ali Ismail, Director of the Department of Zoology; Professor Euclid Bullfinch, Daniel Dunn, Joseph Pearson, and Miss Irene Miller, all of the United States."

Professor Ismail bowed. *"Salaam aleikum,"* he murmured.

They returned his bow. "What does that mean?" asked Danny, always curious.

"It is a way to say hello in Arabic," said Professor Ismail, with a smile. "It means, 'Peace be with you.' "

"It's one of the nicest ways I ever heard," Irene said.

"The only better way," mumbled Joe, "would be, 'Dinner's ready.' "

"But, Joe," said Danny, "we just had a big breakfast on the plane."

"Was that what it was? I thought it was an appetizer," Joe retorted.

Professor Ismail was saying to Dr. Fenster, "All your equipment arrived safely. I suppose you will want to examine it before you leave."

"Yes, that would be best. And what about our permit to conduct investigations?"

"It is waiting for you at the Ministry of National Guidance. I have also made all arrangements for chartering your airplane. It is a land-and-water craft, fitted with drop tanks for extra fuel."

"Splendid, my dear friend. I am very grateful."

"Not at all. It is an important expedition and a very interesting one. I only wish I could go with you this time, but I have too much to do here."

Danny said, "What do you think the *lau* is, Professor Ismail? Could it be some kind of dinosaur? Is that possible?"

Professor Ismail turned his large, kind, brown eyes on Dan. "I do not know what it is, young man," he said. "As for *possible*, in nature all things are possible. Look at this fish, for instance."

He motioned to the tank, and they came closer to peer at it.

Joe said, "It just looks like an oversized sardine. If it had a hard-boiled egg and some mayonnaise with it, I'd be more interested."

"Hard-boiled egg?" Professor Ismail looked bewildered. "I do not understand."

"The boy is a poet," Dr. Fenster said, "and like all poets, he is always hungry."

"Ah, I see. Well, perhaps while we check over your apparatus, these young people could go out and see a bit of the city and have an early lunch."

"Yes," said Danny, "but you started to tell us something about the fish."

"Of course. If I were to ask you if it is possible for a fish to live on dry land, you would say no. No?"

"No. I mean yes," said Danny.

"Yes. Well, this is *Clarias lazera,* a fish that has special air bladders, as well as gills, so that it can come out on land and even live there for long periods of time. It is possible for there to be a wolf which carries its young in a pouch, as the Tasmanian wolf does. Or a mammal which lays eggs, as the duck-billed platypus does. So perhaps it is *possible* that the *lau* is a surviving dinosaur, or a giant water snake, or a creature with tentacles that strikes men dead if they look at it. If it exists at all, it could be anything you like."

"Whew!" Danny let out a whistle. "And we're going to try to find it."

"I'm beginning to hope we don't," Joe said in a small voice.

56

SIX

The Man in White

The expedition's equipment had been stored in a warehouse not far from the University. They all drove there in the big car. The three men began going over the list of materials, opening boxes and crates and checking their contents.

Danny and his friends stood near the warehouse door, breathing in the strange new smells of the city. It looked as though the men had forgotten them in the interest of unpacking.

"Professor Ismail did say we could see the town and have some lunch," Danny said. "Why don't we just take a little walk down this street? Maybe there's a restaurant nearby."

"Why don't we just ask Professor Bullfinch first," said Irene. "I don't want to be a fuss-budget but I don't know enough of the language they speak here to find my way to the corner."

"Girls!" said Danny. "Why are you always so nervous?"

"Pooh to you. I'm right and you know it."

"Girls are always right," sighed Joe. "Okay, let's ask them."

Professor Bullfinch was lifting one of the miniature television cameras out of its case. Danny went over to him and said, "Can we take a walk for a while, Professor?"

Professor Bullfinch pursed his lips. "Well, I don't know whether it would be wise, Dan. I know you must be getting restless, but—"

Professor Ismail interrupted. "Pardon. I remember that they were hungry, particularly the young poet. If I may suggest something?"

"Certainly."

"There is a coffee house not far away, along this street. It is quiet and clean. I know the owner, whose name is Muhammed Rahma. He speaks some English. If the children will go and say to him that I have sent them and that he is to feed them, they can eat and then rejoin us here."

"Great!" Danny said. "Let's go."

"You'd better wait—" said Professor Bullfinch.

"But, why?" Danny cried. "Can't we go? We don't want to stand around here."

"—at least until Professor Ismail tells you

how to find the coffee house," Professor Bullfinch finished drily.

Dan grinned sheepishly. "Sorry," he said. "I forgot about that."

The old scientist quickly explained, and soon the three friends were walking down the hot, dusty street in the bright sunshine. It was wider than the streets at home and there were no sidewalks, but they weren't missed for there were few cars. Many of the shop fronts were open, and they saw a man making a brass bowl in one, while in another a man sat cross-legged, stitching at a shoe with a turned-up, pointed toe. Here and there, people had spread out their wares on the street: boxes of beans or onions, leather slippers, baskets of fish, or lengths of cloth.

They found the coffee house with no trouble. An awning shaded its open front, and when they went inside, it took a moment for their eyes to get used to the darkness after the dazzling sunshine. A fat man in a long white coat came towards them, saying something angrily in Arabic and flapping his hands as if to shoo them out.

"Wait a minute," Danny protested. "We're looking for Mr. Muhammed Rahma."

"Yes, what is it?" the man said. "Who are you? I have no time for jokes."

"Professor Ismail sent us. He said you'd give us some lunch."

At the name, the fat man smiled, showing teeth whiter than his coat.

"Ah, you are friends of his?" he said with a bow. "That is different. Come, sit down. Be wel-

come. But it is very simple here, nothing fancy, not like your American cafeterias. Here, everything is what we say *ahlan wa sahlan*—like in a family."

They sat down on fat-leather cushions around a low table. Mr. Rahma first brought them glasses of cool lemonade. Then he brought out a bowlful of stew, and some pieces of round, flat, soft bread.

"Eat," he said. "And may you have good appetites."

"Well—um—can we have some forks or spoons or something?" Danny said.

"Forks? You have something Allah gave you which is better than a fork. Your hand," chuckled Mr. Rahma. "It is much cleaner. Who knows whether a fork has been properly washed?"

"It's a good thing my mother isn't here," said Joe. "She'd say the same thing about my hand."

They all dipped into the stew with their fingers and with pieces of the flat bread and began eating with gusto.

"Mysterious Africa," Joe said, with his mouth full. "The mystery is, what's in this stew? It's tasty but different."

"Beans," said Mr. Rahma, who stood beaming down at them. "Tomatoes. Garlic. Onions. And goat."

"Goat?" Danny gulped. "Suddenly I'm not so sure it's so good."

"Oh, relax," said Joe. "You must always be ready for new experiences in food. It's not as if it was something like camel."

"Oh, yes, also camel," Mr. Rahma added. "Very nice, eh?"

Joe swallowed with difficulty. "Very nice," he said sadly.

However, they were hungry, and the food, if strange, was really very appetizing. They finished the bowlful and mopped up the sauce with bread. Mr. Rahma brought them some sticky cakes and some tiny cups of coffee, rather muddy but sweet.

"I hope they finish checking over all that equipment soon," Danny said, licking his fingers. "With only two weeks to spend, I'd like to get going."

"I wonder if we really will find anything," Irene mused.

"I'll bet we do," said Danny. "And you heard

Professor Ismail—he said it was important. It'll turn out to be the most important discovery of the century. If there's anything there, Dr. Fenster will find it."

"My own theory," said Joe, "is that it's something from another planet. Remember Dr. Fenster's description? It has long tentacles on its head. A Martian! A spaceship landed a long time ago and the Martian pilot has never been able to get home again, so he's living there in the swamp."

"Neat!" said Danny. "What an imagination. But I'll bet it's a dinosaur—a triceratops, for instance. And the tentacles are probably really its horns."

Mr. Rahma came over to stand beside them. "Is everything, how we say, okay-dokay?"

"Everything was fine," Danny said. "I guess we'd better go now. How much do we owe you?"

"Oh, there is nothing to pay. I will settle with Professor Ismail later. He is a good man, a friend."

The children thanked him and went out into the sunny street. They started back towards the

warehouse. Irene glanced over her shoulder, and
then said in a low voice, "That's funny."

"What?" asked Dan.

"There was a man sitting at the next table in
that restaurant," Irene said. "I noticed him staring at us and when you said something about
the most important discovery of the century, he

leaned over and it looked to me as though he was trying to hear what we were saying. But then I thought maybe I was imagining it."

"When do we get to the funny part?" said Joe.

"The funny part is that he's following us," Irene retorted.

Danny stopped short and looked back. Not far behind was a man in a white suit and a broad brimmed hat. He had a pale, bony face and a thin moustache that turned down at the ends. As soon as he saw that the young people had stopped, he stopped, too. He stood for a moment, hesitating. Then he darted across the street and vanished into a narrow lane.

"It sure does look suspicious," said Danny. "But maybe it's just an accident. Why would he be so interested in us?"

"Maybe he's really interested in Martians," Joe suggested. "And maybe the one in the swamp is his long-lost cousin."

"Well, he's gone now," said Danny. "So there's nothing we can do about it."

They walked on. At the warehouse, they found that the three men had finished and were repacking the equipment.

"A truck will be here soon to take the cases to the airport," said Dr. Fenster. "I'll wait for it, Euclid, and you and Professor Ismail and the kids can go back to the University. Maybe you'd like to have the driver of the car take you on a little tour of the city."

"That would be fine," said Professor Bullfinch.

They went out to the car, which had been parked around the corner in the shade of the building. The driver was asleep behind the wheel. Professor Ismail woke him up and gave him his instructions.

They all piled in. As they drove off, Dan suddenly jerked his head around and stared out of the window.

"What is it?" Irene said.

"That man—the one in the white suit," said Danny. "He was standing in the shadows, back there."

"Are you sure?"

"I'm sure, all right," Danny said. "And I'm sure, too, that he was watching us like a hawk!"

SEVEN

In the Sudd

Getting ready to leave took longer than they had anticipated, and it wasn't until early the following morning that they drove to the airport to board the plane Dr. Fenster had hired. It was a Grumman twin-engine Goose, with a boat-shaped hull and landing wheels.

Danny had told Professor Bullfinch about the man in the white suit. The Professor thought about the matter and said, "I don't believe it was anything sinister, Dan. He was probably just curious about you. After all, it's not every day that three lively young Americans turn up in an out-of-the-way coffee house in Khartoum."

Dan and his friends weren't so sure. All the way to the airport they kept a sharp lookout. But they didn't see the stranger again.

"That doesn't prove anything," Danny said. "He might have been a crook of some kind, or a spy who thought we were trying to discover military secrets. And now he's being more careful."

67

The man in the white suit was soon forgotten, however, as their plane took off, circled over the city and headed south towards the mysterious swampland called the Sudd. They landed briefly at the town of Malakal to refuel. Soon after, the color of the ground below changed from sandy brown to the solid green of reeds, with lines of shining water running among them. Then they saw a wide lake. The plane landed, sending up sheets of water on each side of its hull. It taxied in close to shore.

"I arranged for a boat to come up from the little town of Kodok to meet us," said Dr. Fenster as they unstrapped themselves from their seats. "We'll leave the airplane on the lake, with the pilot, and go west by boat towards Yakwak. My friend Ibrahim saw the *lau*'s track somewhere near there."

The boat was moored to the bank near where the airplane had landed. It had once been a spruce motor launch, but now its paint was peeling and its metalwork was rusty. A man in a turban waved to them from the deck. He went into the wheelhouse, started the engine, and brought the boat close up alongside the plane. His boat

68

might look shabby, but he was obviously very skillful at handling her.

With everyone pitching in and helping, it did not take long for all the equipment and camping gear to be transferred from plane to boat. They said good-bye to the pilot of the plane, who was going to make his own camp on shore and would keep in radio contact with them. Then, to the steady putt-putting of their engine, they glided slowly across the lake. A river opened westward, and soon they had entered it.

The three young people stood in the bows of the boat leaning on the rail. On each side of them rose tall reeds—papyrus—more than twelve feet high, their tops spreading in feathery fans. Now and then, there was a thorny tree with golden flowers among its green leaves. It was called an ambatch. There was little other foliage. Although it was late afternoon, it was blazing hot, hotter than they had ever known. Through the smell of engine oil came another, stronger smell, that of marsh mud.

"It smells *green*," Joe observed.

The river kept winding. Green plants, like lettuces, covered its surface here and there, and

the boat sometimes plowed through masses of
them. A channel opened off to the left, and the
boat, bumping against the soft banks, turned
into it.

Irene pointed. A long-legged bird was wading
near the bank. Its heavy, curved beak seemed
much too large for its head, so that it looked as if
the bird had jammed its head into a Dutch

wooden shoe. As they watched, it took fright and flapped heavily into the air.

"It was a shoebill," said Dr. Fenster, who had come forward to watch. "They're very rare. Some zoos will pay as much as two thousand dollars for one. You were lucky to see it."

"I wish I'd known," Joe said. "I could have jumped out and grabbed it."

"I don't think you'd want to jump out on this shore," said Dr. Fenster. "Look there."

He motioned ahead to what looked like a rough log, lying half in the water, half on the bank. As the boat came closer, the log suddenly slipped off the bank and swam away.

"A crocodile," the zoologist said.

Joe shivered. But Irene said, "How exciting! It's all so strange. Crocodiles and shoebills."

"Yeah," Joe said, with a straight face. "It's almost like being in a foreign country."

Irene gave him a push.

The sun was very low when the boat's engines stopped at last. The river had narrowed. The shores here were dry and covered with grass instead of papyrus.

"The Nuer people burn off the reeds in No-vember, when the dry season begins," said Dr. Fenster. "Then they bring their cattle to graze here. I think they have a cattle camp somewhere nearby."

The boat slid in to the sloping bank. The boatman jumped ashore and tied it up to the roots of an ambatch tree. Dr. Fenster climbed over the railing, and the rest followed. Professor Bullfinch had just set foot on land when Irene gave a sudden squeak.

Three men had appeared as if from nowhere. They were thin, muscular, and so tall that they seemed giants alongside Dr. Fenster and Professor Bullfinch. They wore belts and armbands of beads, and not much else. They had long wooden staffs and stood leaning on them, silently watching the newcomers.

Dr. Fenster said, "*Yibi, yibi.*"

One of the men, whose hair was dyed bright red, replied in a deep voice, "*Yabi, yabi.*"

"*Yi misi juok.*"

"*Ikal, juok.*"

There was silence for a moment. Danny, unable to keep still, said to Dr. Fenster, "What did you say?"

The zoologist replied, "I said, 'Here we are.'

They answered, 'Here you are.' I said, 'May heaven preserve you.' They said, 'And you, too.' "

Unexpectedly, one of the tall men broke in. "Are you English?"

"We're Americans," Dr. Fenster answered.

"Can you speak English?"

"I speak some of your language. And you speak some of ours. That is friendly. What do you want?"

"We want to make camp here."

The tall man shrugged. "No one will stop you."

"Thank you. My name is Fenster. What is your name?"

"I am Cuol, the son of Dar."

"Good. If we want to speak to your people, maybe you will help us, since you know our language."

"Maybe," said Cuol.

"Well," Dr. Fenster said, clearing his throat, "thank you very much. We may as well unload our boat, then."

The three Nuer men stood where they were and watched as the crates and cases were brought to land. The tents were put up: one for Professor Bullfinch and Dr. Fenster, one for Danny and Joe, and a smaller one for Irene. The boatman was to sleep on board his craft. Another large fly tent was put up to serve as a kind of living room and office. The supplies and equipment were left on board for the time being, but Professor Bullfinch set up a portable stove which used bottled gas, and Dr. Fenster and the young people began getting out food for dinner.

Cuol stepped forward and picked up a can. "What is this?" he asked.

"It's pineapple," said Joe. "A kind of fruit. Very yummy."

"Good," said Cuol. "I will take it."

"Huh?" said Joe. "Why?"

Cuol stared at him. "You have much of it and I have none," he said.

"Quite right," Dr. Fenster put in. "Take it. And let your friends take some as well."

Cuol said something to the other two in his own tongue. They each took a can. Then all three, without another word, went silently away into the gathering dusk.

Professor Bullfinch rubbed his bald head. "Interesting people, these Nuer," he said.

"Yes," Dr. Fenster agreed. "I know a little

about them, but not much. Nobody knows much about them, except that they are a Nilotic people who have lived in these swamps for centuries. They are very proud and independent. They have never liked foreigners, and to them anyone who does not come from the marshes is a foreigner."

"They have a good idea about sharing," Joe said. "I'll remember it when we come to dessert."

Dinner was simple: corned beef and baked beans, hard biscuits with canned butter, canned fruit, and coffee. When they had finished and washed their mess kits, night had fallen. A fire would have been cosy, but they had no wood, so they sat in the dark for a while in front of their tents. Professor Bullfinch puffed at his pipe, and Dr. Fenster lit one of his thin cigars.

The night was very quiet. Strange stars twinkled overhead. The air was warm and full of unusual smells. Nobody felt much like talking. They were all very tired and the three youngsters were a trifle homesick.

Suddenly, from somewhere far out in the darkness, came a deep gurgling rumble.

"What's that?" said Danny.

"Lions," Joe said, almost at the same time.

"There are no lions here," said Dr. Fenster softly.

Once again they heard it, fainter this time. It was like the growling of a hungry giant's stomach. It died away and all was quiet again.

"Crocodile?" Professor Bullfinch asked.

"No. That's not the sound a croc makes. Nor a hippo," said Dr. Fenster. "I know them both well."

"Then could it be—?" Danny began, in a voice he could not altogether keep from trembling.

"It's possible," said Dr. Fenster. "It's just possible that we have actually heard the beast we're looking for—the *lau*."

76

Tracks in the Mud

Danny sat up, yawning and rubbing his eyes. Early as it was, the sun was already hot on the canvas of the tent. He gave Joe a shove.

"*Yibi, yibi,*" he said.

Joe groaned. "Too early."

"Come on. We're going to set up the cameras this morning."

Joe struggled out of his light sleeping bag. "Okay. In that case, *yabi, yabi.* I hope breakfast is *yabi,* too."

Dr. Fenster and Professor Bullfinch were already up, and coffee was steaming on the stove. Irene was eating cornflakes with canned milk.

"You're late," she said smugly. "I've been up for hours."

"Well, minutes anyway," said the Professor. "Sit down, boys. We plan to pay a visit to the Nuer this morning, so that there will be no trouble when we set up the apparatus."

"Where's their village?" Danny asked.

Dr. Fenster pointed along the shore. Not far away, they could see pale gray smoke rising. "It's not the village, actually," he said. "That's much farther inland. In the dry season they come down to the river and set up camps. They graze their cattle on the grass, and do some fishing and hunting."

Breakfast didn't take long. Soon, they were following Dr. Fenster along the river bank. They pushed between reeds and tall grasses and came to a fence made of bundles of grass tied together. Beyond it, they could see small huts and windbreaks of grass, with fires in front of them in pits dug in the earth. There were cattle tied up to pegs driven into the ground. The cows were like none they had ever seen. They had humped shoulders and tall, graceful horns.

A couple of children, playing near the water's edge, saw them and ran shouting. Men who had been smoking their pipes around the fires got up and came slowly towards the explorers. Their manner was calm and dignified. After a moment, Cuol, the son of Dar, pushed his way to the front.

Dr. Fenster said, "Good morning. We'd like to talk to your chief."

Cuol smiled. "That will be hard," he said. "We have no chief."

"You mean he is still at your village?" said Dr. Fenster.

"No. I mean there are no chiefs among the Nuer."

"I see. Well, then, who's in charge of things?"

"Each of us is in charge of himself," said Cuol.

Dr. Fenster scratched his chin. "Who gives orders?"

Cuol burst into laughter. "Whoever saw a Nuer come when someone sent for him?" he said. "We do not give orders and we do not take them."

"That is most interesting," said Professor Bullfinch. "Suppose you wanted someone to help you do something difficult?"

"If I needed help, I would say, 'Son of my mother, help me,' and someone would do so."

Dr. Fenster nodded. "Not a bad way to live," he said. "Well, we want to set up some scientific equipment in the swamp. And I wanted to be sure that whatever we did would not interfere with the work of your people. Would you have any objection?"

Cuol turned and spoke to the other men.

After a moment, he said, "We do not mind. You have been friendly to us. If you are foolish enough to put your belongings in the swamp, that is your affair. Only be careful," he added with a chuckle, "that the *lau* does not catch you."

"On the contrary," said Dr. Fenster. "We intend to catch the *lau*, if we can."

Cuol stared down at the bearded little zoologist. Then he spoke to his friends. There was a babble of voices and much laughter.

Cuol said, "We Nuer respect bravery. But you are not brave, you are simply crazy."

"Maybe," said Dr. Fenster calmly. "If the *lau* is really in the swamps, will you tell me where to look for him?"

Cuol said, "You are a foreigner. Why should we tell you?"

Dr. Fenster looked baffled. There was a long moment while he and Cuol eyed each other. Then Danny suddenly stepped out in front of the others.

"Son of my mother," he said boldly, "help us."

Cuol blinked. His haughty expression vanished. He put his hand over his mouth, but his eyes twinkled.

"I cannot say no to that," he said. "Especially as your hair is the same color as mine. Very well. I will go with you and show you where the *lau* sometimes comes out of the water. But I will be sorry when you are all dead."

"You won't be half as sorry as we will," Joe muttered.

Cuol explained to the other men what had been said. He got his staff and prepared to go with the explorers. All at once, shouting broke out from the crowd.

The cause of the trouble was Joe. He had noticed an earthenware pot of milk on the ground next to one of the fires. He had walked over boldly and was just about to drink from it when one of the men saw him and, grabbing his arm, began to scold him in the Nuer language.

"Joe!" said Professor Bullfinch. "What on earth are you doing? Put it down."

Joe shrugged. "On the way here you told us to respect the customs of other people, didn't you, Professor?"

"Well, of course. But—"

"I'm just doing what they do. Cuol helped himself to pineapple last night and said, 'You have much of it and I have none.' Well, they have lots of milk and we only have that canned stuff."

"He is right," Cuol said. "We Nuer like people who stand up for themselves. You are foreigners, but I like your children. Drink, boy," he added to Joe.

Joe tipped up the pot. Next moment, he was spluttering and coughing while milk dribbled down the front of his shirt.

"It's sour!" he cried. "Ooh, it's horrible."

Professor Bullfinch patted him on the back and handed him a large handkerchief.

"If you really want to follow the customs of the country," he said mildly, "you ought to drink it all. But perhaps there's a limit to how far one can go."

They returned to their boat. They had a couple of rubber dinghies with them, which they now inflated. With these, they could get about more easily and more silently than with the big boat. Cuol got into one with Dr. Fenster and Danny, while Professor Bullfinch, Joe, and Irene took the other.

They paddled across the river. On the far side, the reeds still thrust up more than twice the height of Cuol, tall as he was. There were many

winding little waterways threading among the reeds. Cuol chose one of them, and Dr. Fenster marked it by sticking a thin metal rod with a small white flag on it into the bank.

They followed the waterway for some distance, and then Cuol stopped paddling and said in a low voice, "Do you see that stump?"

Ahead, the stream divided. In the center, there was a point of land on which was a jagged, dead tree stump.

"That's the place, is it?" asked Dr. Fenster. "That's where you have seen the *lau?*"

"I have never seen the *lau,*" Cuol replied. "If I had, I would probably not be here now."

"Then how do you know it comes out of the water there?"

"I know."

Professor Bullfinch had brought his rubber boat up alongside Dr. Fenster's. He said, "Tell me, Cuol, is the *lau* real?"

"Real?" Cuol seemed perplexed. "Of course he is real. He is as real as any evil spirit."

"As any—? I don't understand. Is he a spirit?"

"I do not know. He is the *lau*."

Professor Bullfinch mopped his dripping forehead. "Ben," he said, "I have a feeling we're on a wild-goose chase."

"You mean a wild-spirit chase, don't you?" said Dr. Fenster. "Maybe you're right. Tell me, Cuol, is the *lau* alive the way we are?"

Cuol shook his head. "He is alive, but not the way we are."

Dr. Fenster sighed. "All right. Let's go look at that spot."

They paddled to the fork and got out, pulling their boats up on land. The ground was soft near the water and they moved with care. They spread out, looking at Cuol for guidance.

"Somewhere here . . ." Cuol murmured.

Then all at once, two things happened.

Joe gave a wild yell and jumped straight up into the air, slapping at his thigh. And Irene uttered a muffled shriek.

"I'm bitten!" Joe bawled. "Help! Snakes! I'm dying!"

He was making so much noise that they ran to him first.

"Where is it? Where are you bitten?" asked the Professor.

Joe took his hand away from his thigh.

"I can't see any wound," said Dr. Fenster. "And it's sort of high up for a snakebite."

Cuol smiled. He bent over and picked something off the ground. He held it out on his palm. It was a large horsefly, squashed flat by Joe's slap.

"*Seroot,*" he said.

"Of course," said Dr. Fenster. "I might have known. It's one of the few savage beasts here in the marshes. I forgot to warn you about it. It's not poisonous, but it bites like anything."

"You're telling me," Joe groaned. "It felt like a red-hot needle."

Professor Bullfinch glanced at Irene. She was

85

standing quite still. She had been a little ahead of the others and on the end of the line, near one branch of the stream.

"Were you bitten, too?" asked the Professor.

She shook her head. "Come over here," she said in a strained voice. The others joined her.

There was a deep furrow sloping up from the water into the soft soil. The reeds and grasses had been smashed down and the earth churned into a trench so wide that all six of them could have stood in it, side by side.

Something had come ashore there and then gone back into the water, something so big that they found it hard to imagine.

NINE

On the Monitor Screen

The rest of the day was spent in the hard work of setting up their observation post.

The portable generator was unpacked and assembled. It was small, but powerful enough to provide all the electric power they needed. A number of plastic balloons were inflated from a helium cylinder. Three miniature television cameras, using about a hundred watts each, were fastened to the balloons. Three special infrared lamps were also attached to balloons. They would show up anything that came into their field at night, but would not disturb it.

This equipment was ferried over to the triangular point of land where they had seen the strange marks. They cut down reeds and cleared a space so that they could work more easily. Cameras and lights were hooked up with Professor Bullfinch's new superconductor. The plastic cord was as light as spider web and not much thicker, so that hundreds of yards of it could be unreeled without dragging down the balloons. The balloons were allowed to soar to a height of about thirty feet and tethered with lengths of the plastic line pegged into the ground, so that they couldn't float away. The cameras now scanned a large triangle of swampland.

The superconducting lines were then led back to camp where the final hookup was made to the control panel, the generator, and the television monitor screens. The plastic cord needed no support, as wires or cables would have required.

The generator was started, and they tested the equipment. On their monitor, the patch of ground with the river running along both sides of it showed up clearly.

"It's a lucky thing we have you kids with us," said Dr. Fenster. "With five of us to share the job, we can keep a fairly continuous watch on the television screens."

"Do you think the creature will show itself in daylight?" asked the Professor.

"Since we don't know what it is, there's no telling," Dr. Fenster said. "But whenever it comes—if it does—we'll try to be ready for it. I'll work out a schedule."

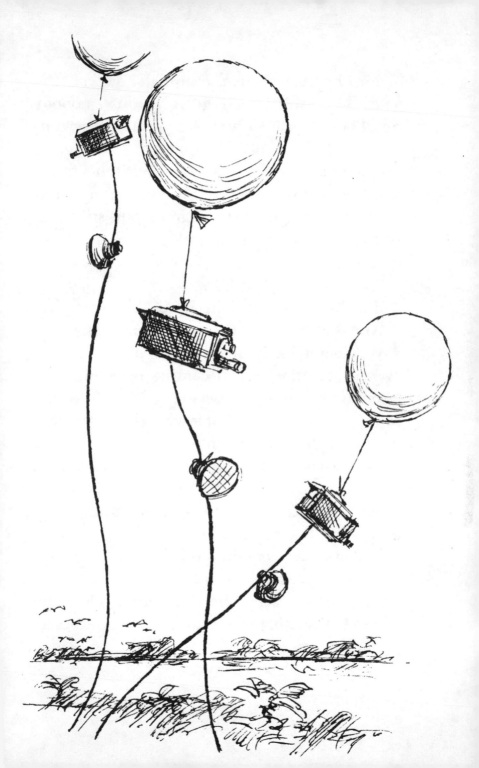

For the rest of that evening, however, the schedule wasn't much good because nobody could bear to tear himself away from the screens in case the *lau* suddenly appeared. The young people finally crawled away to their tents in exhaustion at midnight. Danny was up again at the very first light. He staggered out, still half-asleep, and found a bleary-eyed Professor Bullfinch seated before the TV screens.

"Anything?" asked Dan.

The Professor shook his head. "Nothing yet."

And that was to be the pattern for the next six days. They took it in turn to watch, and after every watch the person coming on would ask, "Anything?" and the person going off would reply, "Nothing yet." At night, the three children took the hours from nine to midnight, and the two men divided the remaining six hours or so from midnight to dawn. They all began to look, and feel, very worn, as much from disappointment as weariness.

When they were not on duty, they passed quiet and peaceful hours dawdling along the river bank or visiting the Nuer camp. The Nuer assured them that there were no crocodiles in this part of the swamp—"The *lau* has eaten them all," they said. However, they did not venture to swim, though they did feel they could

walk or fish along the shore without fear. Joe rigged a hook and line and pulled in some perch, which they had for dinner and found delicious. Irene made friends with some of the Nuer girls, who were rather shy of her at first but soon responded to her warm and sympathetic ways. They taught her how to milk the hump-backed cows, which was their main job. In return, she got a long piece of heavy line and taught them the mysteries of skipping rope. They all went crazy about the game, and so popular did it become that Irene found herself loaded down with presents from grateful admirers: beaded belts and ivory bracelets. As for Danny, whose curiosity could never be satisfied, he became very friendly with Cuol and began to learn a little of the Nuer language. He also learned how to throw the long spear with which the men fished, and once or twice he was allowed to go hunting for small game with Cuol, who called him "Brother Redhead."

But time was passing, and everyone began to feel the strain as no further trace of the *lau* appeared. Their monitor showed nothing but empty swamp. After a time, Dr. Fenster considered moving the cameras to another spot.

He and Professor Bullfinch were talking about it one day, as the Professor's watch was ending.

Breakfast had been eaten, and Danny had just come to take over the first two hours of the morning.

"I'll give it one more day," Dr. Fenster said. "Then we'll move."

"Gosh, then we won't see our friends here any more," Danny said sadly.

"Oh, I don't plan on moving the base camp," said Dr. Fenster. "I'm thinking of just shifting the cameras and monitor screens. Euclid and I will go deeper into the swamp and set up an observation post there."

"What about us?"

"You all seem to be getting along so well with the Nuer, we thought we'd leave you here to look after our base."

"Oh, no!" Danny wailed. "What's the good of that? Then we won't be around when you catch the *lau?*"

"*If* we catch it," Professor Bullfinch amended. "It doesn't seem very likely right now, does it?"

"But—but—" Danny stuttered, "but you'll be all alone, just the two of you. How can you handle a thing that big by yourselves?"

Dr. Fenster raised his eyebrows. "If it exists and it's really so big, I'd rather not have you three enthusiasts underfoot. I didn't intend to let you come along if we saw it on the screens, my lad. And in any case, I don't intend to tackle it with my bare hands. I'll have Little Sandy to help me."

"Who's Little Sandy?" Danny asked.

Dr. Fenster patted the holster he wore on his belt. "Little Sandy's my portable Sandman," he said.

He unsnapped the flap of the holster and pulled out a strange-looking pistol. It had a long thick barrel and an unusual cylindrical grip.

"It's a specially modified air pistol," he explained. "It's very powerful, and instead of shooting bullets, it shoots a dart containing a new tranquilizer drug. It is guaranteed to put an elephant to sleep. It ought to deal with our friend the *lau*."

He replaced the pistol and closed the holster. "I suspect, however," he went on, "that the *lau* is going to turn out to be either a big python or an oversized crocodile. Everything points to one or the other. So you won't miss much by not seeing it the moment it appears."

"But—" Danny began.

Professor Bullfinch patted him on the shoulder. "Don't fuss, Dan," he said. "You'll have to leave it to Dr. Fenster to make the decisions. He's the boss of our expedition."

The two men went off, leaving Dan alone with the monitor. Glumly, he stared at the familiar scene which appeared on the three small screens.

Tall reeds swayed gently, bordered by dark water. Nothing else. Danny sighed.

But it would be much worse if the Professor and Dr. Fenster went off by themselves tomorrow. There wouldn't even be the hope of excitement.

"We might as well go home right now," Danny mumbled.

He broke off, holding his breath. Surely, something was moving on one of the screens? He touched a dial to sharpen the focus.

There *was* something there. A small boat had nosed in to shore. A man got out and took a few steps. He stopped and stared upward so that he was looking directly into the lens of one of the cameras.

There was no mistaking him in spite of the small size of the picture. Even the white suit was the same. He was the man who had followed them in Khartoum.

TEN

"Sabotage!"

Danny sprang to his feet. Another glance at the
screen and he ran to find the others.

"Professor Bullfinch! Dr. Fenster!" he shouted.
"Come quick!"

The Professor had just fallen asleep in his
tent. He came rolling out, almost bringing the
whole tent down. Joe and Irene had set out to
visit the Nuer camp, but they came hurrying
back when they heard Dan's shouts. Dr. Fenster
had been reading, and his book went flying.

They clustered around the monitor. But now
the screens were empty.

"He was there," Danny insisted. "I recognized
him."

"But why?" said Professor Bullfinch. "It
doesn't make sense. Could he have followed us
all the way here?"

"Let's go take a look at the spot," Irene said.
"If he was really there, we'll see the mark of his
boat or his footprints."

"A good idea," said Dr. Fenster.

They all went down to the shore. But before they could get into the rubber dinghies, they heard the sound of an outboard motor. Out of

the winding waterway that led into the swamp came a boat. A man sat in the stern steering. And in the bow seat was the man in the white suit.

"I don't understand this," Dr. Fenster murmured. "Why didn't we hear him before? He must have gone past this spot on his way into the swamp."

"Maybe he didn't want us to hear him,"

Danny said softly. "He could have shut off his motor and used paddles."

"True."

The motorboat came straight to where their own launch was moored. The man in the white suit stepped out on land.

They could see that his white suit was wrinkled and dirty. His sallow face had a sly air. His sharp eyes flitted over the group and came to rest on Dr. Fenster.

"Good morning," he said. "I see the famous explorer Benjamin Fenster, *Mtu'anaye,* do I not? I introduce myself. Jean Canigou, at your service."

He bowed. Dr. Fenster, tugging at his beard, did not return the bow, but said, "What do you want?"

"Only to help," said Canigou. "My work brings me to the Sudd sometimes. And here I come and I see your balloons floating in the air. Very surprising."

"No doubt," said Dr. Fenster. "It must be very interesting work that brings you into the Sudd."

"Very interesting, indeed. I am a collector of rare animals. So I know much about the country

and how to find and catch all different species."

"I see. And what makes you think you can help us?"

"Dr. Fenster jokes me," the other man said, rubbing his hands together. "You have long talks with Professor Ismail, and you come with your equipment to this place. Everyone knows that Dr. Fenster is famous for catching animals."

"It sounds to me as though you have been spying on us," Dr. Fenster said sternly.

Canigou shrugged. "I only know what everyone knows. Something very big, very important, a new animal, maybe the most important discovery for many years."

Irene nudged Danny. "That's what he heard you say," she whispered.

"So perhaps I can help?" Canigou continued.

"Perhaps not," said Dr. Fenster. "Thank you very much. We don't need your help. I suggest that you go now. Good-bye."

Canigou lost his friendly expression. His face became cold and hard.

"Maybe you will change your mind," he said.

"I doubt it," said Dr. Fenster.

Canigou stepped back into his boat and spoke a word to the other man, who started the motor. The boat swung away from land and went off downstream.

"Well!" said Professor Bullfinch. "A most interesting encounter."

"I know that man," said a deep voice behind them.

It was Cuol. He had come up without their hearing him, and he was standing on one leg with the other drawn up so that he looked like a stork. It was the peculiar way in which the Nuer rested.

He went on, "He is a bad man. He cheats and steals. I have even heard that he will kill if he wants something badly enough."

"Hmp!" grunted Dr. Fenster. "A delightful fellow. If he's an animal collector, I'm the king of Spain."

Cuol said, "He has made camp a half mile or so down the river. He has other men with him."

"What do you think he's after?" asked Professor Bullfinch.

"He sniffs money," said Dr. Fenster. "Remember the shoebill we saw? I told you how much some zoos will pay for one. You can imagine how much Canigou might get if the *lau* turned out to be the biggest python ever seen—and he could get his hands on it and sell it."

"Dear me," said the Professor. "What do you think we'd better do?"

"At the moment, nothing. So far, all we have of the *lau* is a noise in the night and some marks in the mud which might or might not mean anything. I suggest that we go on with our watch for the rest of the day, anyway."

102

"Yipe!" said Danny. "I forgot. It's still my turn."

He made for the monitor. A moment later, he was calling for help again.

"Don't tell me you've seen another snooper," said Professor Bullfinch.

"The fact is that I can't see anything at all," said Danny.

All three screens were blank. The Professor examined them and looked over the control panel.

"Very odd," he muttered. "Nothing seems to be wrong."

He went to inspect the generator. After a moment, he uttered an exclamation.

"It's blown!" he said.

"What do you mean?" asked Dr. Fenster.

"It looks as though it was shorted out. The insulation has failed and the generator is burned out."

The two men plunged into a technical discussion. Finally, the Professor said, "Well, unless we can figure out a way of fixing it without the proper parts, we have no power. It's just possible the fault came from the cameras, although I don't see how. We'd better go check them."

They all piled into the rubber boats, for the young people didn't want to be left out. They paddled to the point where the dead tree stump stuck up. Before they even reached it, they could see the balloons holding cameras in the air above the heads of the papyrus. There were only two of them.

They hauled their boats up and walked to the spot where the third camera balloon had been anchored.

The river bank here was scarred and churned up by marks very much like those they had seen before. The TV camera lay half-buried in the mud. There was no sign of the balloon.

Dr. Fenster and Professor Bullfinch bent over the camera.

"Someone's pulled it down," said the Professor.

"Maybe it was the *lau*," Joe said. "Maybe he didn't like being a guest star on TV."

"I'll tell you what it is," said Danny. "It's sabotage! And I'll bet you anything the man who did it was that fellow Canigou!"

ELEVEN

The Monster of the Swamp

"You may be right," Professor Bullfinch said slowly. "But why? What could he hope to gain from such a thing?"

"He knows what we're after," said Danny. "And he wants to catch the *lau* himself. So he pulled down our camera and did something to it that blew out the generator."

The Professor shook his head. "Doesn't quite make sense, my boy. Why only one camera?"

"He didn't have time to do more. Or he got scared. Or he decided that wouldn't work and then came to see if he could join us. Or—"

"Too many 'ors' and none of them quite fits," said the Professor. "What do you think, Ben?"

Dr. Fenster was staring into space. His eyes held a blank, distant look.

"Is that so?" he said vaguely.

"Ben—"

"Not at all," said Dr. Fenster. "Get in touch with me on Wednesday."

He turned his back, clasping his hands behind him.

"Ah, well," Professor Bullfinch said, "we won't hear from him again until he's thought through whatever he's thinking about."

He picked up the camera and studied it with a frown. "It's scorched, as if it had been struck by lightning," he said. "The question really is not how this happened but what to do about it. Without electrical power our search for the *lau* has come to a dead end."

"I have an idea, Professor," Irene said. "We could make a—well—a kind of burglar alarm."

"First he's a TV star and now he's a burglar," said Joe. "No wonder nobody knows what the *lau* looks like."

"I mean," said Irene, "we could string a cord all around this place and tie the ends of it to a couple of cooking pots. When the *lau* comes ashore, he'll pull the cord and down will come the pots."

"We'd be kind of far away to hear the noise, wouldn't we?" Danny objected. "Why don't we all camp here and wait?"

"Great!" Joe said. "Why don't you all camp

here and I all go back to the Nuer camp and see what's for lunch?"

"Well, we could do both," said Irene. "I mean, camp here and also put up the alarm signal so we'd be warned."

"Now, now, just a minute," Professor Bullfinch interrupted. "I am certainly not going to allow you three to wait here for the *lau*. If anything happened—"

"But Professor!" said Danny. "You've always told me that a scientist should always let his curiosity be greater than his fear. Haven't you?"

The Professor fiddled with his pipe. "I can't deny it. But on the other hand—well, let's see what Ben has to say."

He looked around. "Ben?"

There was no trace of the zoologist.

"What's happened to him?" said the Professor.

Danny peered at the ground. "Here's a footprint," he said. "He must have wandered off deeper into the swamp."

"Perhaps—" the Professor was beginning.

Without waiting to hear the rest of it, Dan said impetuously, "Don't worry. I'll go find him."

He dashed off into the high reeds, for he had

seen another footprint in the black earth. He thought he saw, too, where the papyrus stalks had been pushed aside and broken. He hastened in that direction. The ground was firm and there were no more footprints, but he pressed on. After a time, the reeds thinned. He came out abruptly on the edge of a small pool where tall grass grew around still, brown water.

He could hear the distant voices of his friends, calling. But where he was, all was very quiet.

The stems of the reeds rose about him. They were three times his height—a thin, whispering, feathery forest. They were the same in every direction. Above, the sun pulsed in a brilliant sky, sending down burning waves of heat. A small bird with a long tail and a bright scarlet breast darted close, hovered for a moment over the pool, and shot away again.

Danny opened his mouth to shout, "Dr. Fenster!" but his voice trailed away after the first sound. There was something menacing about the sameness of the reeds and the hot silence of the air.

Again, he heard someone calling faintly. It sounded very far away.

"I'd better get back," he thought. It wasn't

that he was really scared, he told himself, but only that it was silly to get separated from the others.

Now, where was it he had come from? He saw a place where some of the reeds had been broken and started off that way. But after a moment, there was no further sign of a trail. "I'll go back to the pool," he thought, "and start again." He retraced his steps, trying to find his own tracks, but mistaking other marks in the soil for footprints and getting mixed up when he found breaks in the reeds in several different places.

He stopped. He could no longer hear his friends. He couldn't find the pool. Every place looked like every other place here, and there were no landmarks.

"Oh, gosh," he groaned. "What a dope! Headstrong, always acting without thinking. Now what?"

He stiffened. In the quiet, he could distinctly hear a soft rustling among the reeds. Then he could see the shadow of some large thing moving. It was hard to make it out because of the shifting light among the reed-stems.

He was poised, ready to run like mad, when a voice said, *"Yabi, yabi."*

"Cuol!" Danny exploded in relief.

The tall man parted the last few stalks and grinned out at him.

"Oh, man! Am I glad to see you," Danny said.

"And I am glad to see you, Brother Redhead," said Cuol. "Come. Follow me."

He led the way through the reeds. Danny said, "How'd you happen to be here?"

"Some of my kinsmen told me that the man, Canigou, is planning to come with spearmen and make his camp near your camp. I came to warn your people. They told me you were in the swamp."

They soon emerged to join the others. "You've got him, I see," Professor Bullfinch said. He looked rather pale in spite of his sunburn.

He shook his head at Danny. "My boy, you really must learn to restrain yourself."

"I'm sorry, Professor," Danny said earnestly. "I won't ever do anything like that again. But where's Dr. Fenster?"

"He still hasn't returned."

Cuol said, "I will go now and find him."

But before he could move, there was a loud splashing in the river.

Cuol froze. Professor Bullfinch began to say

111

something, but the Nuer raised a hand commandingly for silence.

They all stood, waiting. Another splash, and then the ground beneath their feet trembled.

They glanced at each other. Shivers ran up and down Danny's spine. Looking at the faces of his friends, he could see in them the same sudden terror he was feeling.

The reeds swayed wildly and then were flattened. Irene screamed. A gigantic shape, like something out of a nightmare, heaved itself into view.

They had a glimpse of an enormous round head, gray-black and shining, of waving tentacles as long as a man's body, of a stiff crest rising behind them.

For a moment that seemed to stretch on forever, the monster remained motionless. The five people stood as if paralyzed. Then Cuol bravely raised his long staff and took a step forward.

"You others—run!" he said.

Rashly, Danny drew his hunting knife. All he could think of was Cuol's courage. He ran to the Nuer's side, determined to help him.

Someone bellowed, "Stop!"

114

Dr. Fenster burst out of the reeds behind the group.

"Get back!" he roared. "Quick! If you so much as touch that thing, you're done for!"

TWELVE

"You Have One Hour"

His shouts broke the spell. The monster's head reared up again, and it began to move.

The group burst apart and fled. Danny had a glimpse of Dr. Fenster pointing the heavy air pistol he called Little Sandy. He heard a snorting and rumbling, and then he tripped and fell headlong. He lay struggling to catch his breath, and at last rolled over.

Dr. Fenster stood there calmly, pistol in hand. "It's all right," he said.

Dizzily, Dan sat up. The others were coming out of various hiding places among the reeds. Dr. Fenster slipped his pistol back into the holster.

"Two darts, well placed," he remarked. "I think the *lau* will nap for a while."

He glanced at Cuol. The Nuer had not run with the others but had only moved back a few paces.

"You're the bravest man I know, Cuol," Dr.

Fenster said. "But thank heavens you didn't touch that thing."

He turned and walked up to the beast. Professor Bullfinch and Cuol followed. Dan scrambled to his feet, his curiosity getting the better of his fright.

The *lau*'s thick, snaky body was longer than a two-ton truck. Its skin was smooth and glistening. It had no limbs, but two fins grew from behind its great round head, and it had used these as forelegs. Another fin, which they had taken for a crest, ran down its back almost to the flat rounded tail. Its mouth split the bottom of its head from side to side—a mouth large enough to gulp down a man. What they had thought were tentacles were actually long spiny whiskers that grew from around its lips and now lay limp on each side of the body.

"It looks like—" Danny began. "I can't believe it, but it looks like—"

"A catfish!" Joe exclaimed. "It looks like an overgrown version of one of those little bullheads we used to catch in Moffat's Pond."

He reached out to touch the dark wet skin. Dr. Fenster snapped, *"No!"*

Joe jumped. "I was just going to see what it felt like," he said.

"It would be the last thing you ever felt," said Dr. Fenster.

Professor Bullfinch pushed his glasses farther up on his nose. "You don't mean—" he said in surprise. "A *Malapterurus!*"

"A related species. I'm sure of it."

"I can't believe it."

"Nevertheless, there it is," Dr. Fenster said with satisfaction. "A twenty-foot-long electric catfish!"

"Electric?" cried Danny.

"Exactly," said Dr. Fenster. "If you touched it, you'd be electrocuted. It's difficult for me to say without tests, but I should guess from its size that the thing can discharge a thousand volts or more."

Joe's mouth had dropped open. "An electric fish?" he gasped. "I never heard of such a thing."

"I have," said Irene. "There's an electric eel, too, isn't there, Dr. Fenster? I think it's found in South America."

"There are electric fish in many parts of the world," replied the zoologist. "Some live in fresh water and some, like the electric ray, live in the ocean."

"But how is it possible?" Joe asked.

"All nervous and muscular tissues generate tiny electric currents," said Professor Bullfinch. "Your brain, for instance, puts out as much as one ten-thousandths of a volt. In some fish there are special cells called electroplaques, which are hooked up in series and can build up quite a respectable voltage."

"But this thing comes out on land," Danny said, looking up at the giant form which lay quietly before them. It somehow no longer looked quite so threatening now that they knew what it was. "Is it really a fish?"

"Don't you remember the fish Professor Ismail showed you?" said Dr. Fenster. "There are several varieties of the catfish family that have air sacs which allow them to live for a time on dry land. I'm not surprised that this specimen has them. What surprises me is that it took me so long to realize what the *lau* was."

He shook his head. "I should have guessed. It shows you how easy it is to have all the information you need before your eyes and yet not see what it means. The Nuer were right—the size and color and snaky body are all there, and even the long 'tentacles' which aren't tentacles at all but feelers that every catfish has around its mouth."

"And even the part about 'If the *lau* sees you first, you die!' " said Irene with a shiver.

"That's right. Not just a quaint legend, you see, but a very real possibility. It explains why there are no crocodiles in this region. The catfish's electricity can act as a defense or as a way of killing its prey. The electric organs are all over the fish's body, just under the skin.

"I knew there were electric catfish in Africa," Dr. Fenster continued. "They are found in many parts of the upper Nile, and in rivers right across the continent. The natives call them 'thunderfish.' However, they're generally less than a foot long, although one or two specimens have been found running to as much as four feet. I just never connected them with the *lau*. But Joe was right, you see."

"Me?" Joe said. "What'd I say?"

"You said that maybe the *lau* knocked down the camera. And when Euclid said something

120

about 'struck by lightning' that started me thinking. Something might have come ashore, tangled with the superconductor, and accidentally pulled down the camera, tearing off the balloon in the process. The next logical step, of course, was that it might have been something capable of sending an electric charge back to our generator. And if there had been a fault in the insulation of the generator, it would have blown."

They all looked with respect at the *lau's* motionless body.

Irene said, "But if it's asleep, can it still hurt us?"

"Oh, yes. Its discharge is an automatic reflex and would respond to a touch, or a poke."

Cuol had been listening carefully to everything that was said. Now he put in, "So that is the *lau*. I have heard of it all my life, but I never thought I would see one. And you have not killed it but only put it to sleep?"

"That's right," said Dr. Fenster.

"Then you are a fool. Why don't you kill it? When it wakes, it will kill you."

"No," said Dr. Fenster. "It won't harm you if

121

you don't touch it. And I want to study it."

He took off his broad-brimmed hat and scratched his head. "I'm afraid I didn't prepare for *this*, though. We certainly can't take the *lau* away with us. We'll measure it, photograph it—"

"We've got a portable voltage meter with us," Danny said. "We ought to find out how much of a charge it puts out."

"Exactly, my boy," said Dr. Fenster approvingly.

Professor Bullfinch had been walking around the giant creature. Now he said, "We're going to have a bit of a problem keeping it, Ben. We can't build a cage that will hold it."

Joe said, "We're going to have another problem, Professor. Maybe even more serious."

"What is it, Joe?"

"Visitors," said Joe with a jerk of his head.

Jean Canigou's boat was approaching. They had all been so interested in the *lau* that they hadn't noticed the sound of the motor.

Canigou stood in the bow. There were five other men with him, one of them steering the boat. They were dressed in ragged clothing and wore dirty turbans or skullcaps. They were armed with spears and clubs.

"They are bad men," said Cuol. "They are from a village farther up the Nile."

The boat coasted to a stop and Canigou sprang ashore. His eyes widened as he saw the *lau*. He walked up to the explorers and stopped.

"I see you have had some luck," he said. "That is a fine catch. What is it?"

"That's none of your business," Dr. Fenster answered sharply.

"But it *is* business, good business," said Canigou with a thin smile. "Much money, if such a strange big fish can be sold to the right person."

"It's not going to be sold," said Dr. Fenster. "Suppose you get back in your boat and leave us alone."

Canigou scowled. "Suppose you think about this," he said. "We are six men with weapons. You are two men and three children. I don't count him—" he motioned to Cuol. "He has nothing to do with this. I don't want trouble, but I am going to take that thing, whatever it is. I will go now. I will wait downstream. You can have an hour to think about it. You think carefully. Maybe you don't want those youngsters hurt, eh?"

He stepped into the boat. As it moved away, he called over the noise of the motor, "One hour. Then I come back and take it."

THIRTEEN

Danny Finds an Answer

Joe broke the long silence. "He didn't even say please," he muttered.

The others couldn't help smiling, in spite of the tension.

"But it's no laughing matter," said Professor Bullfinch. He took out his pipe and slowly began to fill it. "That man's dangerous."

"We can't risk the lives of these three," Dr. Fenster said, nodding at the young people.

"Oh, you are so right," said Joe quickly.

Danny said indignantly, "You're not going to let Canigou get away with it, are you?"

"If you want a simple answer," said Joe, "yes."

"Professor! Dr. Fenster!" Danny cried. "We can't! We discovered the *lau*. And now he'll just take it—"

"Why don't we let him?" said Irene thoughtfully. "I mean, let him come and try to move it. He doesn't know it's electric."

"I see what you mean," Dr. Fenster said. "He'd be in for a shock."

"We can't allow that," Professor Bullfinch said gravely. "Someone might be killed. We would have to warn him. Well, wouldn't we?"

They nodded.

"No, that's not the answer," he went on. "I think Danny's got a real point. We just shouldn't let Canigou get away with this. But I don't see how we can stop him."

Irene said, "Maybe Cuol would help?"

"That's right!" Danny turned to the tall Nuer. "Would you, Cuol? Couldn't you get some of your people and help us stop Canigou?"

Cuol slowly shook his head.

"It has nothing to do with us," he said. "The *lau* is deadly. Why should we care who has it?"

Dr. Fenster sighed. "That's it, then. I don't see that we have any choice. I can't think of a way of preventing that fellow from doing what he wishes. How much time have we left, Euclid?"

Professor Bullfinch drew back his sleeve and glanced at his watch. Before he could answer, Dan gave a screech that made everyone jump.

"*Watch!*"

126

"Watch what?" said Professor Bullfinch.

"Watch where?" Dr. Fenster said, looking around.

"Not where. Watch!" spluttered Danny. "Which watch. I'm sorry, I mean wrist watch. That's it. That's the answer."

"Poor lad," said Dr. Fenster in an undertone to the Professor. "He's frightened out of his wits. He doesn't know what he's saying. We'd better get him out of here, and the sooner the better."

Danny was dancing about in a frenzy of excitement. He seized the Professor's arm.

"I'm *not* frightened out of my which—I mean, wits," he cried. "Listen! Don't you remember when you discovered the superconductor? You couldn't get your hand past the magnetic field because your watch was caught and held. Why can't we set up the same kind of field and stop Canigou?"

Dr. Fenster began, "I told you he's—"

But Professor Bullfinch held up a hand and stopped him. "Wait a second, Ben. This isn't as crazy as it sounds. If Canigou has any metal on him, he'll have a hard time getting past such a field. And there's no telling what effect a strong magnetic field might have on the human brain. I don't know whether it would work, but it's certainly worth a try."

Then the animation faded from his face. "Drat! We've forgotten. We haven't any power supply. Our generator's broken. And even if it

weren't, how could we transport it from our
camp to this spot and get it going in time? No,
I'm afraid it's no use. It was a good thought,
Dan, but without any electrical power—"

He broke off.

Danny, with a wide grin, was pointing to the
lau.

FOURTEEN

The Invisible Barrier

"We will need," said Professor Bullfinch briskly, "about fifty feet of copper wire. If we can get back to camp, perhaps we can unwind the armature in the generator."

"That won't be necessary," Dr. Fenster said. "I have a coil of copper wire in one of the boxes. I brought it along not for any scientific purposes but for trading. I find that many people I meet like it for bracelets and necklaces."

"Fine! You'd better go back to camp and get it. And hurry. We have about fifty minutes left, and it will take you most of that time to get there and back."

"What if you meet Canigou?" said Irene. "He said he'd wait downstream while we made up our minds."

"Yes, he might make trouble."

Cuol said, "I will do this for you—I will show you a quick way on the other side of the river, through the reeds."

Dr. Fenster gripped the Nuer's shoulder. "Thank you, Cuol," he said. "Let's go. There's no time to lose."

He and Cuol shoved off in one of the rubber boats. Professor Bullfinch and the young people could do nothing but wait. The Professor, trailing blue smoke from his pipe, took out a notebook and began jotting down a description of the giant catfish as calmly as if he were in his own laboratory.

Danny said, "Aren't you afraid, Professor?"

"Of Canigou? I suppose I am. But there's no point in spending any time over the matter," said the Professor, "since there's nothing I can do about it at the moment."

He began pacing the length of the fish.

"I wish I could be so cool," said Joe. "But I guess I'm just a fool." He stopped, and a look of surprise came over his face. "Cool, fool, school. Ha!" He fished in his pockets, brought out a scrap of paper and a pen, and began scribbling.

"So that's what they call inspiration," said Irene. "Isn't it marvelous, Dan? I wish I could do it."

131

Joe went on muttering to himself. At last, he read aloud:

> The day was very calm and cool,
> And I was on my way to school,
> When with a loud and wet boo-hoo
> A mournful fisherman came in view.
> He said, "I went down to the brook;
> Into the current dropped my hook.
> I hoped for something for a meal
> And caught a large electric eel.
> And now although I'd like to try him,
> I haven't any place to fry him."
> "Plug his tail into his head
> And let him cook himself," I said.
> He gave a sob of utter joy,
> And said—

"Here comes Dr. Fenster," said Danny.

"That doesn't rhyme," Joe objected.

"I know. But it really is Dr. Fenster and Cuol. They're back."

The two men landed, while Professor Bullfinch looked at his watch and remarked, "That took less time than I thought it would."

Dr. Fenster had a coil of copper wire and another of the plastic superconductor. He and the Professor at once bent to their preparations.

On the ground, they laid a circle of superconductor about twenty feet in diameter. Parallel to this and just touching it they made a winding of several loops of wire. They led one end of the wire back to the *lau*.

The Professor said, "Everybody inside the circle, please."

When they obeyed, he used Cuol's staff—which, being wood, was a non-conductor of electricity—and carefully pushed the free end of wire up to the *lau* until it was in contact with the creature's skin. Then he lifted the staff and gave the *lau* a sharp poke.

After a few seconds, Joe said, "Well? When does something start happening?"

"I hope it has already happened," said the Professor. "An electrical charge should have passed from the fish into the copper winding. The winding should have transferred its momentary magnetic field to the superconductor, which should now be functioning as a permanent and powerful magnet. I hope."

He walked to the rim of the circle with his hand outstretched. At the same time, they all heard the noise of Canigou's boat.

"It's all right," said the Professor hastily. "Now, stand still and stay inside the circle. Let's hope this works. If it doesn't—"

"I'm good at surrendering," Joe mumbled.

Canigou and his men clambered ashore. Canigou's jacket was open and beneath it they could see a heavy curved dagger on his belt. He rested a hand on its hilt and surveyed them.

"I hope you have decided," he said.

"We have not decided," said Dr. Fenster. "But the *lau* has."

Canigou looked blank. "The *lau*—?"

134

Dr. Fenster said, "The *lau* is more than a fish. It is a spirit. It is the spirit which has lived in this place for thousands of years. It will not go with us nor will it go with you. We have agreed to leave it alone, and it has promised to protect us. You cannot harm it or us."

He then rapidly repeated the same thing in Arabic, so that the other men could understand. They shifted uneasily and murmured to each other in low voices.

But Canigou said, "Do you think I'm a fool? I don't believe you."

"No?" said Dr. Fenster. "Then tell your men to throw their spears at us."

He did not wait for Canigou to do so, but pointed at the nearest of the man's ragged followers and barked a command in Arabic.

The man raised his spear uncertainly. At an angry word from Canigou, he drew back his arm and hurled the weapon.

Straight at Dr. Fenster it flew. But it never reached him. It stopped in mid-air. It hung there for a moment, and then its shaft slowly sagged. It sank down, butt first, until it lay flat on the ground.

A second man threw his spear. It, too, stuck

fast in the air and seemed to float to the ground.

The others dropped their weapons. They uttered a groan of terror and dismay.

With a snarl, Canigou whipped out his dagger. He rushed at Dr. Fenster. His men saw him run and then come to a dead stop. It was as if an unseen barrier were holding him back.

He tried to force himself forward. He looked like a man leaning against a high wind. The explorers, staring at him, saw his face change from fury to bewilderment. Then, as he bent over, trying to push his dagger against the invisible shield, he came into the full power of the magnetic field. A strange expression came over his features. As Joe later remarked, "He looked as if he had his head caught in a lemon-squeezer."

He let go of the dagger, which remained hanging in thin air. He staggered backward, fell, and lay still.

"Is he—?" Irene began fearfully.

"Just unconscious," said the Professor. "I can see him breathing."

Dr. Fenster spoke sternly in Arabic to the other men, who were huddled together, their eyes wide with alarm. Two of them came nervously to pick up Canigou. They dragged him to the boat, rolled him in, and jumped in after him.

The motor started. As the boat pulled away, one of the men pointed back to shore and shouted something.

"I think that's the last we'll see of Canigou," said Dr. Fenster in a pleased tone. "We've given him and his men something to think about."

Danny grabbed him by the sleeve. "Look, look!" he yelled.

A deep gurgling rumble made the zoologist whirl.

The tranquilizer had worn off. The *lau* was waking up.

FIFTEEN

Farewell to the Lau

The great fish reared high. Its long barbels, or whiskers, waved like branches in a breeze.

The explorers shrank back. There was no time to flee.

But they need not have feared. The *lau* heaved itself around. Its immense tail flapped over their heads, just missing them. With a couple of giant wriggles, it reached the river. In it went with a splash that showered the little group.

"Gone!" said Danny.

He started to follow, but the Professor caught his arm. "Don't move," he warned. "Have you forgotten when happened to Canigou? We don't know what the magnetic field actually did to him, but it couldn't have felt very pleasant."

He took Cuol's staff. "I must ask a great favor," he said. "Do you mind if I break this in half?"

"No," said Cuol. "Break it if you must."

The Professor put it across his knee and tried. After a moment, Cuol took it back and with one sharp movement snapped it.

Professor Bullfinch kept one piece and gave the other to Cuol, explaining what they had to do. They reached out, each with his piece of wood, and managed to push the two ends of the circle of superconductor apart.

There was a violet flash and a *crack* as the spark jumped the gap. Then the Professor picked up one end of the superconductor and began coiling the strand.

The three youngsters ran to the river's edge. There was no trace of the *lau* except for a few widening ripples.

"And you never even got a chance to photograph it," Danny said to Dr. Fenster. "No one will believe we really saw it."

"That doesn't matter, my lad," said the zoologist cheerfully. "Professor Ismail will believe me. He and I will come back with the proper equipment for studying the creature. Meanwhile, Cuol, perhaps you and your people will keep an eye on this spot. And when I do return, perhaps you will help me find the *lau* again."

Cuol nodded. "You have done a strange thing," he said. "I do not understand it. Is the *lau* indeed a spirit?"

"No, it's all perfectly natural. I just can't explain it to you at the moment."

"I see. Well, when you come again, look for me here or at the village of Yakwak. And," he added, "don't concern yourself about Canigou. If he ever shows himself here again, I and my brothers will send him on the wrong path."

They collected the cameras and the lights and loaded them into the dinghies. They were all sobered by the excitement of the past few hours. They paddled slowly and quietly down the river until their tents came in sight.

"It's funny," Danny said, when they stood on land once more. "I'm going to miss this place. It's all so strange, and we've only been here a short time, yet it seems familiar and sort of homelike."

Irene looked out across the river at the feathery fronds of papyrus. "In a way," she said, "I hope they don't catch the *lau*. It wouldn't be happy in a zoo or anything. It would miss this place, too. It belongs here."

"Yes," Dr. Fenster said. "We will try to observe it if we can, rather than catch it. Because it is so large, and so dangerous, there can't be many of them. It will be important to preserve them. That's another reason we must try to keep Canigou from returning. I'll discuss the matter with Professor Ismail. I'm certain he can get the authorities in Khartoum to do something."

Professor Bullfinch puffed thoughtfully at his pipe. "Long ago," he said, "a great naturalist wrote, 'Out of Africa always come new things.' We've seen one of the strangest of them today."

Joe nodded. "Yes, well, when we get home, we'll see a new thing that came out of our country—something Africa can't match."

"What do you mean, Joe?" asked the Professor.

"Ice-cream sodas," said Joe with a sigh of anticipation.

About the Authors

JAY WILLIAMS, co-author of the Danny Dunn books, has been a professional writer for the past twenty-eight years. To his credit are twenty-five fiction and non-fiction titles for children of all ages, in addition to the twelve books about Danny. Parents, teachers, librarians, reviewers, and especially little children have found *The Cookie Tree, The Question Box, Philbert the Fearful,* and *The Practical Princess* memorable and enchanting tales. Mr. Williams also has an enviable reputation on both sides of the Atlantic as an author of adult novels of which *Uniad* (Scribner's) is the most recent. Born in Buffalo, New York, he was educated at the University of Pennsylvania, Columbia University, and the Art Students' League. Now, Mr. Williams and his family live in England—where perhaps at this very moment, he is reading a letter from a young fan who has written to suggest the plot of the next suspense-filled scientific adventure for their hero, Danny Dunn. RAYMOND ABRASHKIN authored and co-produced the very popular and successful "Little Fugitive" which won an award at the Venice Film Festival.

About the Artist

PAUL SAGSOORIAN was born in New York. He studied art at several art schools in New York City, and also went to the Map Making School of the U.S. Army. In 1957, the American Institute of Graphic Arts selected a book illustrated by Paul Sagsoorian as one of the Fifty Best Books of the year. Mr. Sagsoorian has been freelancing since he completed his art training. Now, he works for art studios, advertising agencies, and book publishers.